HOME
COURT

BY JAKE MADDOX

text by
Steve Brezenoff

STONE ARCH BOOKS
a capstone imprint

Jake Maddox is published by Stone Arch Books, an imprint of Capstone.
1710 Roe Crest Drive
North Mankato, Minnesota 56003
www.capstonepub.com

Library of Congress Cataloging-in-Publication Data is available on the Library of Congress
website.

ISBN: 978-1-4965-9700-7 (library hardcover)
ISBN: 978-1-4965-9916-2 (paperback)
ISBN: 978-1-4965-9751-9 (eBook PDF)

Summary: Lew loves playing on the Westside Community Center basketball team. He is
shocked when he learns that the community center might be shutting down, jeopardizing
the future of the team. With no school teams available to them, Lew and his friends worry
they won't get to compete in basketball at all. Can Lew and his teammates find a way to
keep the center open and give their team the opportunity to win big on their home court?

Designer: Dina Her

Image Credits
iStockphoto: FatCamera, cover; Shutterstock: Brocreative, (grunge) design element, cluckva,
design element, Lane V. Erickson, (basketball) design element

Printed and bound in the United States of America.
PA117

TABLE OF CONTENTS

CHAPTER I

TIP-OFF

Lew Garrison wiped the sweat from his forehead with the back of his hand. It was just a practice scrimmage with teammates, but he still wanted to win.

Of course Lew and his friends played basketball for fun mostly, but winning always felt pretty good. This season, their team was in the city playoffs. It felt like a spot in the finals was almost in the bag.

"You're going down," said the boy across the half-court line. Nico D'Ano had four inches on Lew and a strong vertical jump. He was also Lew's best friend.

Bonsa, who was about the same height as Nico, faced off against Nico for the tip-off.

Lew was pretty sure Nico would win it. But Lew's scrimmage team could make up for it later. They were faster.

Sam Duran, also known as Coach Sammy, blew his whistle. "Ready," he said, and he tossed the ball straight up between the two players.

Nico leapt up and tapped the ball backward to his teammate, Lew's other best friend, Anang Benjamin. Anang was one of the best ball handlers on the Westside Community Center basketball team, the Wasps. He also had a great three-point shot, so Anang often played shooting guard while Lew took the point guard position.

Playing for the Westside Community Center Wasps was the only way these boys could play on a real basketball team. Their own schools didn't have teams, but the WCC Wasps played official games against local schools that did have teams.

Lew and Anang went to a small middle school with almost no sports, clubs, or after-school activities. Nico's school on the south side of the city couldn't afford a team.

In three paces, Lew hurried to Anang and put on the pressure. His teammates fell back a little to cover Nico and the others.

"You're not going anywhere," Lew said with a grin.

"Watch this," Anang said. He faked dribbling right, then left, and then pivoted around Lew. With two steps and one bounce, he shot a pass right back to Nico.

Lew was fast, but not fast enough to stop it. Nico caught the pass and spun around a defender for a layup. Two points.

Nico and Anang high-fived.

"Nice play," Lew said, patting his friends on their shoulders. "Hey, Coach Sammy. Did you see—"

But Coach Sammy didn't see. He paced on the sideline with his cell phone to his ear.

"He's been on the phone almost the whole practice," Nico pointed out.

"What's that about?" Lew said.

Anang shrugged.

"You guys playing?" called a teammate from under the basket. He was ready to throw in the ball to start the game again.

"Sorry," Lew said. "Let's go."

* * *

After the scrimmage, Lew grabbed his towel from the bench and wiped his face. Coach Sammy was still on the phone.

Lew joined Nico and Anang at the line for the water fountain outside of the gym.

Out in the main room of the community center, there were still loads of balloons and ribbons up. There had been a fundraiser there a few nights ago. A sign hanging over the front desk read *SAVE OUR CENTER.*

All the boys' parents and family friends had been there for carnival games, snacks, and a late-night movie in the gym. Anang's big sister even won the raffle at the end of the night for a free dinner for four at Lew's favorite Mexican restaurant.

"I don't think Coach saw more than ten seconds of that scrimmage," Nico said. He nodded toward Coach Sammy just inside the gym doors. He was sitting in a folding chair now with his head in one hand and the phone at his ear.

"I hope everything's okay," Anang said. "It's not like him to ignore practice like this."

Lew nodded. The team was as important to Sammy as it was to the boys. He'd even played on the Wasps when he was young.

As they watched him, he hung up the phone and slipped it into the pocket of his track jacket. He stood up and sighed. When he noticed the boys looking at him, he smiled—obviously forced.

"Hey, Wasps," Coach Sammy said with one loud

clap of his hands. "Get hydrated and then meet me at the bench. I've got some big news to share."

Though he was thirsty, Lew didn't wait for his turn at the water fountain. He grabbed Anang's elbow and pulled him back into the gym. Nico followed. Pretty quickly, so did the rest of the Wasps.

"Find a seat, boys," Sammy said as he paced in front of the bench. He didn't look any of them in the eye as they sat down.

"Spit it out, Coach," Anang said.

"Yeah," Lew said. "Whatever it is, we can handle it. You quitting or something?"

Sammy shook his head. "Never," he said. "I'm never quitting on the Wasps."

"So what's up?" Lew said.

"You were all at the fundraiser this past weekend," Sammy said. "You know it went about as well as anyone could have hoped."

"Yeah," Nico said. "My mom said we raised a ton of money for the center."

Sammy frowned. "A ton, maybe," he said. "But if we did, we're still a ton short."

Lew's stomach dropped. A shiver ran through his body. "Short of what?" he asked.

"The fundraiser this year was more important than any of us knew," Sammy said. "At least anyone who doesn't sit on the parks and rec board."

"So what's the deal, Coach?" Anang said. "Do we need to hold another fundraiser?"

"I'm afraid it's too late for that," Sammy said. "For now, we'll keep holding practice and playing in our games, but in a week, the Westside Community Center will close, and the Wasps will cease to exist."

CHAPTER 2

THE LIFE

Practice was over—soon it would be over for good—but the three friends' day of basketball wasn't over yet.

"Dominic has the life, man," Lew said as he and his friends walked up the front path of the nearby private school, White Rock Academy. Dominic Davis, the fourth member of their group of friends, was a student there. The building's front was two stories of clear glass. Three huge LCD screens hung just inside and showed highlights of the Waverunners' basketball season.

Lew, Anang, and Nico stood there a moment and watched. Parents and students moved around them on their way to the gym for the game.

"There's Dominic," Lew pointed out as their friend's highlight came up.

They watched the familiar clip of their friend. He spun past a defender, faked a shot, passed to a guard in three-point range, and then hurried into the paint. The guard passed the ball back to him. In one smooth move, Dominic grabbed the pass, ducked under a jumping defender, and put down a layup.

"He's good," Nico said.

Lew and Anang nodded.

"I'm better," Nico added with a grin.

The boys laughed and hurried into the big gym.

The stands were already mostly full. The cheerleading squad was at center court in the middle of their pregame routine. The pep band sat in the front rows of the bleachers. They played the school's song, brass and drums booming out with pride.

The boys found seats in the first row of bleachers near the door. As they sat, Dominic spotted them and hurried over.

"Hey, thanks for coming, you guys," Dominic said as they all slapped hands. "I thought you had practice."

"Just came from there," Lew said. "We ended a little early."

"Yeah," Anang said. "Everyone was too depressed to play."

Lew told Dominic about Coach Sammy's bad news.

Dominic shook his head. "That stinks," he said. "What are you gonna do?"

The WCC boys looked at each other.

"Nothing," Nico said with a shrug.

"Yeah," Lew said. "What can we do?"

"That's totally unfair," Dominic said. "Meanwhile, White Rock is about to get a brand-new scoreboard as nice as the one at the city arena."

The old scoreboard hung over center court.

"That one seems okay to me," Lew said, looking up at it.

Dominic shook his head, grinning. "The new one will have four screens. It'll show different angles throughout the game, as well as highlights and replays. It's gonna be awesome."

"And it will probably cost more than the whole community center is worth," Anang said.

The Waverunners' coach called Dominic back to the bench.

"I gotta go, guys," he said. "Enjoy the game. And then get out there and start selling candy bars or something to raise money!"

He fist-bumped his friends and then hurried back to his team.

Lew stared at the old scoreboard as its big screen cycled through the Waverunners' starting lineup.

"Sell candy bars," he muttered to himself. "Gimme a break."

CHAPTER 3

SAVING THE CENTER

"Maybe he's right," Anang said the next morning. "I've seen kids at the mall selling candy bars to raise money for stuff."

Lew, Nico, and Anang sat on the grass next to the outdoor court at the park. They'd been playing there all morning, since there was no official practice scheduled.

The boys kept the community center building at their backs so they wouldn't have to look at it. They didn't want to think about how it might close soon.

"Do you have a thousand candy bars in your pocket?" Lew said.

Anang didn't answer. It was a pretty silly question.

"How about a bake sale?" Nico said. "My dad's brownies are the bomb."

"My mom will take any opportunity to force her cinnamon rolls on anyone within a hundred miles," Lew said with a shrug.

"We might as well try," Anang said.

"Let's go talk to Ms. H.," Lew said. "Maybe we can have it in the center." The three boys jumped to their feet and ran into the center.

* * *

"Sorry, boys," said Ms. Handel, the woman at the desk inside the center. "I can't let you sell homemade food inside the building."

"Why not?" Lew asked.

"Yeah," Nico said. "It's for a good cause!"

"Don't you want the center to stay open?" Anang asked.

Ms. Handel smirked at him. "Honey, this is my second home," she said. "I'd do just about anything to keep it open. But what I can't do is have the health office down here dragging three middle school boys and me off to the precinct for selling food without a license."

Feeling defeated, the three boys went back outside. Lew held his basketball under one arm.

"We don't *need* the building," he said. "We can set up anywhere."

"Like, just on the sidewalk?" Nico said.

Anang shook his head. "Nuh-uh," he said. "We're not babies selling lemonade. I'm not doing that."

"No one said 'babies,'" Lew said. "It's a nice day for March. A thousand people will be out walking past my building. They'll want a drink. And brownies smell good."

"Cinnamon rolls smell good," Nico added.

"Fine," Anang said. "When?"

"Today," Lew said. "We can get set up before folks are leaving work." He bounced the ball a few times, passing it between his legs smoothly.

"We'll meet in front of your house, then," Nico said. "You got a table?"

Lew nodded. "Anang, you bring the lemonade," he said.

"Why me?" Anang complained.

"Because your mom and dad don't make brownies or cinnamon rolls," Lew said. "And don't forget the ice."

They bumped fists and hurried their separate ways.

* * *

A few hours later, everything was ready.

Lew set up a table with three chairs and a cooler on the sidewalk. He hung one sign that read

SUPPORT YOUNG ATHLETES and another that said
SAVE OUR TEAM.

Nico's dad's brownies were amazing. The
cinnamon rolls' smell brought in passersby from all
over the neighborhood.

A hot afternoon sun pitched in. Everyone wanted
some lemonade.

When the streetlights switched on around seven,
the boys' plastic bucket of money was overflowing.

"I can't believe how well this is going," Anang
said.

Lew beamed with pride. "We're actually gonna
make it," he said.

Dominic—their friend who went to White Rock
Academy—walked up with two of his friends from
school. The three private school boys were still in
their uniforms from Saturday practice, and still
sweaty.

"Work up an appetite?" Lew said as he poured
three cups of lemonade. "Still a few treats left, and

plenty of lemonade."

"Sure, thanks," Dominic said. He took out a few bills. "How much have you guys made?"

Nico shook his head. "It's bad luck to count it before you close," he said. "But look at this." He held up the bucket of money.

Dominic whistled, impressed.

But the boys next to him laughed.

"Knock it off," Dominic said under his breath.

His friends didn't care.

"They should hear the truth," one of them said.

Lew recognized him as Silas Preston. He'd played pretty well in the game last night.

"What's that supposed to mean?" Nico asked Silas.

The third boy, Teo, downed his lemonade in one go. "Ahhhh," he said. He wiped his mouth with the back of his hand. "It means," he said, grinning like a panting dog, "that unless that bucket is full of hundred- and thousand-dollar bills, you're not even close to having enough."

Lew felt his face get hot. He realized he didn't even know how much money it would take to save the center. Details like that hadn't seemed important.

"I heard my mom and dad talking about the center this morning," Dominic said. He looked at his shoes. "The center owes over twenty thousand dollars, guys," he said.

"You're lying," Anang said.

Dominic shook his head. His two friends laughed even more.

"This isn't all we've raised," Lew said quickly. It was a lie, but he felt so stupid—so childish—to have thought that he, Nico, and Anang could raise enough money to save a whole community center just by selling brownies and lemonade.

"Good," Dominic said, smiling. He held out a ten-dollar bill.

"You already paid," Nico said.

"I know," he said. "This is a donation to the

center, that's all."

He didn't want his friend's charity, but the truth was they needed it. Reluctantly, Lew took it.

"Ha," Silas said. "Like that'll get them over the top."

"Yeah," said Teo. "The funny thing is, even if you save the center, you'll still have to play in that hundred-year-old gym with those rickety baskets."

"Why don't you guys just get outta here," Nico said.

Lew could feel his embarrassment and sadness turning into anger—rage, even. If the White Rock boys didn't clear out soon, he'd dive across the table and punch one of them, he was sure of it.

"Come on," Dominic said. He put a hand on each of his friends' shoulders and moved them away. Then he turned to Lew, Anang, and Nico. "See you guys at your game on Monday, okay? I'll be cheering for you."

"Sure," Lew said through gritted teeth. He'd

forgotten they had a game on Monday evening against Riverside Middle School.

He wasn't sure there was a point in continuing to play. The team wouldn't even exist when the season ended.

CHAPTER 4

QUARTERFINAL

Coach Sammy paced in front of his team in the Riverside Middle School visitors' locker room. "I know it seems hopeless," he said. "And I know that no matter how well we play today, we won't play in the finals."

Lew's heart sank. His skin went cold.

"What do you mean?" Lew asked. "This is the quarterfinal. We'll be closer to the finals when we win, right?"

"Yeah. Even without the center," Nico said, "we can still *play*, right?"

Coach shook his head. "I'm afraid we can't afford to be in the finals," he said. "There are league fees, court fees, and three refs to pay. We already owe the league back payments for the last four weeks of the season.

"We're lucky the league is letting us play in the playoffs," he went on. "The coaches over at White Rock pushed hard to shut us down right away. The league compromised with them to let us play up until the finals, but not in the finals. White Rock says it's not fair to let a team who can't pay league fees take home the trophy."

Lew sagged on his bench and shook his head.

"But the Wasps I know play because they love the game," Coach Sammy went on, "not because they want some shiny trophy at the end of the season."

Lew leaned forward and put his elbows on his knees. "A trophy would be nice, though," he said. "If this is gonna be it for the Wasps, it would be nice to go out with a bang."

The other boys on the team nodded.

"True," said Coach. "But short of a miracle, this team won't exist when the finals come around. So let's get out there today and play as hard as we can. Not because we want that spot in the finals, but because we love the game."

"You got it, Coach," Lew said.

The boys got up from the bench.

"Huddle up," Coach said. He put his hand in the middle of the huddle. The players added their hands too.

"For the love of the game," Coach said. *"Go Wasps!"*

* * *

Nico took the game-starting tip-off with a tapped pass to Lew.

Lew drove hard up the court, passed to Anang, and moved toward the hoop to set a pick on a Riverside defender.

Anang dribbled to the top of the key. He faked a shot and passed to Nico.

Nico cut under the hoop and went in for the layup. The ball rolled around and out of the rim. Lew jumped for the rebound and passed it to Anang at the top of the paint.

Anang took a shot—a swish for two points.

"Nothing but net," Nico said, slapping Anang's hand. The team hurried back on D.

The Riverside River Dogs set up a 1-3-1 offense. Their point guard launched a pass to the right wing. Anang put on pressure, and the wing passed back to the top of the key.

The point guard tried to fake to the hoop and pass to the forward under the boards, but Lew was too quick for him. He knocked the pass away and followed the ball into a fast break.

Two River Dogs hustled back and posted up on the blocks, but Lew passed to Anang, who took the layup for two more points.

Lew and Anang high-fived. "We got this," Anang said.

"Don't get cocky!" Coach Sammy said from the bench. He clapped a few times. "Keep the defense strong and keep up the teamwork, boys!"

* * *

The Wasps led the game through to the fourth quarter. The River Dogs got within six points, but when there were just a couple minutes on the clock, it looked like a win was in the bag for the Wasps.

With just a few seconds left, Nico caught a rebound and quickly passed to Lew, who drove to the hoop. Two River Dogs fouled him on the shot.

The ref blew her whistle. The teams lined up for the foul shots.

"Just for fun, Lew," Nico said from his place alongside the key. "No pressure at all. We've got the game."

"Yeah," said a River Dog posted up across the key. "The whole game is just for fun, since you won't make it to the finals no matter what happens."

Lew's eye twitched as he released the ball. It bounced off the back of the rim with a thud.

The same River Dog under the basket put his hands to his mouth like a megaphone and shouted, "Brick!"

Lew sucked his teeth as the ref handed him the ball for his second foul shot.

He raised the ball to shoot.

"What are you going to do with those ratty old uniforms?" said the same bigmouthed River Dog. "Maybe you can use them as rags when you get a job cleaning bathrooms."

Lew took his second foul shot, but his anger made him miss again. This time the ball soared under the rim, fluttering the net and bouncing into the stands behind the hoop.

"Oof," said the bigmouth. "Maybe it's for the best you Wasps won't be in the finals."

Lew charged him. He dove at him, wrapped his arms around his middle, and knocked him into the folding chairs under the basket.

"Fight! Fight!" shouted some kids in the stands.

The River Dogs' wise guy jumped up and pushed Lew in the chest. Lew knocked him backward again. Spectators hurried out of the way as the boys tumbled together into the stands.

Nico grabbed Lew by the arm to pull him off. Anang held back the River Dogs' loudmouth.

The ref blew her whistle. "Out," she said, pointing to Lew and then to the boy on the River Dogs. "Take a seat. Technical foul. Riverside, two shots."

Lew shook off Nico and Anang and stalked to the bench. He sat down. Sammy put a hand on his shoulder. "Not a good way to finish," the coach said.

"I know," Lew said. He shook off Coach Sammy's hand. "He asked for it."

The River Dogs' best shooter took the technical foul shots. He sank both, bringing the score to 64–60.

There were only a few seconds left. The Wasps—minus Lew, plus Austin, his sub—brought the ball slowly up the court to run out the time.

They won the game, so they won the quarterfinal, but somehow to Lew it didn't feel like much of a victory.

CHAPTER 5

A NEW PLAN

On Saturday morning, Lew and his big sister, Ro, walked to the park.

"Nico and Anang are probably there already," Lew said. "Can't you walk any faster?"

"If you're in such a hurry," Ro said, "feel free to walk ahead."

Lew clicked his tongue.

"Besides," Ro said, "what's the rush? You don't have anything to do today."

"Practice," Lew said.

"You practice every day, all the time," Ro said.

"And we gotta sell more lemonade and brownies and Mom's cinnamon rolls," Lew went on.

He spotted Anang and Nico at the park's outside basketball court. They were already playing a game of one-on-one.

Ro's friends were sitting together on the swings, waiting for her. They'd catch a bus to a movie at the mall from here.

She shook her head. "You're wasting your time, you know," she said. "You'll never get enough just selling stuff to people on the street."

"So we're just supposed to give up?" Lew said.

"Of course not," Ro said as they hurried across the park drive and stepped onto the grass. Nico and Anang stopped their game and walked toward them.

Ro's friends hopped off the swings.

"But you don't need a bake sale or anything like that to save the team," Ro continued. "You need a *sponsor*."

Ro's friend Wanda put an arm around Lew's shoulder. "Yeah, little man," she said.

He shook her off.

Wanda laughed. "When the high school choir wanted to take a trip to New Orleans for the competition," she said, "we got a bunch of sponsors. They paid for our flights, our hotel, our uniforms . . ."

"Wow," Nico said. "Maybe she's right."

"Maybe?" Ro said. "I have never been wrong."

Lew thought it over. For the money they still needed, it would take thousands of cups of lemonade to even come close.

"Here's my idea," Ro said. "You guys forget practicing for today. Ride the bus to the mall with us. Talk to the businesses there."

"Appeal to their sense of local pride," Wanda said.

"It could work," Anang said. "I'll call Coach Sammy and make sure it's okay for us to ask for sponsors."

"All right, I'm in," Lew said. "Let's go."

* * *

Most of the stores were just opening when the boys started walking around the mall. Anang said Coach Sammy had seemed doubtful they'd get the funds they needed, but he gave the boys his blessing to try.

They skipped the big national stores and focused on the local businesses, hoping the owners would know of the community center and would want to support it.

Their first stop was Top Scorer, a small chain of sports stores with one store at the mall and another on Main Street.

The three boys walked toward the counter.

"How are you boys this morning?" said the man at the counter. "I see you already have a basketball. Anything I can help you find?"

"Actually, we're here to ask you about basketball," Lew said.

"We play for the Wasps," Nico said.

"The Westside Community Center team," Anang added.

The man nodded slowly. "Yes, I've heard of you," he said. "I live nearby."

"Great!" Lew said. "Then you probably also saw we had a big fundraiser down there a couple weeks ago."

"The thing is," Nico said, "we didn't raise enough and—"

"Say no more," said the man, putting his hands up. "I'll be happy to make a donation."

"Well, actually," Lew said, "we're looking for something a bit more than that."

The man frowned at him.

"The fundraiser came up very short of what we need," Lew went on. "Now it'll take sponsors to keep the community center—and the Wasps—going."

"Ah," the man said. "Well, we've never sponsored youth sports before. It's probably a good idea. Why don't you have your coach get in touch with me, and I'll help you out with uniforms and gear. Sound good?"

The boys looked at each other.

"I know it's not much," the man said, "but I run a small business, and times have been tough. I'm sure if you keep at it a few weeks, you'll get together enough sponsors to keep your center."

Lew put out his hand. "Thanks," he said as the man shook it. "We appreciate it."

The boys headed back into the mall.

"A few weeks," Nico said. "We don't have a few weeks."

If they'd started months ago, maybe they'd have had a chance. But with just a handful of days until the center would close, finding enough money in time would be impossible.

CHAPTER 6

WASPS VS. WAVERUNNERS

On Saturday evening, the Wasps played their semifinal game against the White Rock Waverunners.

Because of a Rock Creek Rockets win the day before, that team already had a spot in the finals. It was between the Waverunners and the Wasps for the other spot.

But everyone knew that whoever won today, the Waverunners would likely take the spot in the finals. The community center had only three more days to pay its bills, or the Wasps would be forced to leave the league. They wouldn't exist for the final the following weekend. Today's game would be their last.

It was fitting that the game took place at Westside Community Center. It might not have been the best court in the league, but it was theirs—home court, at least for now.

"The last game at the center," Coach Sammy said to the team right before the tip-off. "Let's make it a good one."

He didn't need to give the same speech again. Everyone knew the game wouldn't mean much as far as a trophy was concerned. But they would play their hearts out.

The bleachers at the community center were only eight rows high and ran along only one side of the court. It wasn't like the impressive seating at White Rock's home court. But the bleachers were full of fans: friends and family of the players and employees of the community center.

Lew also spotted a few people he'd met at the

lemonade stand the other day. He even saw the owner of Top Scorer.

Nico faced off against Silas for the tip-off. Silas got a finger on the ball just in time to knock it to Dominic.

Dominic took point position at the top of the key. He passed off to Silas, who pushed through for a layup.

He missed the shot. Nico grabbed the rebound and fired it up the court to Lew.

Lew started into a fast break, passing it off to Anang as he crossed the center line. He glanced down at the painted yellow jacket on the wood as he hurried to post up.

Anang passed across the paint to Bonsa on the right wing. Bonsa got it back to Lew, who had cut to the top of the key.

Lew found Nico under the backboard and passed it high.

Nico jumped and laid it in for the first two points of the game.

The home crowd went crazy.

Silas threw the ball inbounds and found Dominic. Dominic dribbled up the court. He raised one hand in a fist to signal the play.

Teo, the third boy who had come to the lemonade stand with Dominic, posted up.

Silas jogged around behind Dominic and darted toward the basket. Dominic passed. Silas grabbed the ball out of the air and laid it up.

The ball rolled around the rim and dropped off the side. Nico took the rebound and fired it off to Lew. Lew started the fast break, found Nico under the basket, and passed.

Nico put up the easy layup. The score was 4–0.

The first half was close, but the Wasps held on to a six-point lead. Lew's speed, Nico's height, and Anang's outside shot all proved too much for the Waverunners.

Though their friend Dominic was a strong point guard and sank a few great outside shots, it wasn't enough.

At the end of the third quarter, Anang got cornered and tried for a tough three-pointer.

He missed. Nico grabbed the rebound and tried to put it back up. Silas blocked Nico's shot and knocked the ball to Dominic.

Dominic broke downcourt. He faked to the lane and dropped back. Silas came around for the pass, stepping into the paint.

Dominic passed, leading Silas to the easy layup. But Silas's shot rolled around the rim and dropped off the side. Another miss.

"That's not fair!" Silas yelled. "The rim is bent. Why else would I miss that easy layup?"

"He's right, ref!" the Waverunners' coach called across the court. "This court isn't up to league specs."

CHAPTER 7

SEMIFINAL SURPRISE

The ref blew her whistle. She jogged to the sideline and talked to the White Rock coach.

"If my player says the rim is bent," the coach said, "then it's bent."

The ref blew her whistle again and put up a *T* with her hands for time-out. "All right, let's get a ladder out here," she said.

"This is ridiculous," Lew said as he sat on his team bench with the rest of the Wasps. "Silas misses a few easy shots and blames the hoop."

"So let them check the rims," Coach Sammy said. He paced in front of the bench. "You know the ref is an honest woman. She'll get the game back on in a minute."

While the ref climbed up to examine the rim, Lew kept his eyes on the White Rock bench. Silas looked so smug there, standing behind his team with his hands on his hips.

He was even laughing.

"Something funny, Silas?" Lew said as he leaned forward on the bench.

"Plenty," Silas said, grinning at Lew.

Coach Sammy put a hand on Lew's shoulder to tell him to keep quiet. But Lew shook it off.

"Remember what happened the other day," the coach said. "You ended up getting ejected from the game."

But Lew barely heard him. "Go ahead!" Lew shouted. "Tell us what's funny!" He stood up and stepped toward the other team's bench.

The whole crowd was silent. The ref inspected the rim, while everyone else in the gym watched Silas and Lew.

"Lew, ignore him," Anang said. Lew felt Anang's hand on his arm. "Just let it go."

Silas laughed. "This court is funny," he said. "It's crooked and warped, and the paint is peeling and faded."

Lew gritted his teeth.

"The rims are bent," added another boy on the Waverunners. "The nets are ripped."

"Shut up, guys," Dominic said.

"No, he wants to know what's funny," said another White Rock boy, smiling at Lew. "Another funny thing is that the league ever let the Wasps play when you're not even part of a school athletic program."

Lew clenched his fists so hard that his fingernails dug into his palms.

"But the funniest thing of all," said Silas, "is that even if you win this game by fifty points, you're still not playing in the finals."

Lew's vision went red.

"Because in less than a week," Silas taunted, "this stupid community center will be knocked down."

Lew dove at the other bench.

Silas dove right back at him.

The boys fell to the floor, wrestling.

The ref, who had come down from the ladder by now, blew her whistle over and over, as loud as she could.

Lew felt Silas's fist in his stomach. He grabbed at Silas's wrists and tried to pin him down.

Nico and Anang grabbed Lew and pulled him off of Silas.

Dominic took Silas by the shoulders and dragged him back to the Waverunners' bench.

"You," the ref said, "and you!" She pointed firmly at Lew and Silas. "Out of the game, and out of uniforms. You can watch the game from the stands."

Lew pulled away from his teammates. He made

eye contact with Coach Sammy for an instant.

He could see disappointment in his coach's eyes. But he could also see something else—something like shame.

It made Lew even angrier. He was about to start in on the Waverunners again when Dominic walked up to the ref.

"I'm quitting," he said.

"What?" said one of the White Rock boys. "You can't quit!"

The Waverunners' coach walked up. "What's this about, Dominic?" he asked.

"Nothing personal, Coach Jenssen," Dominic said. "But the rest of the team just showed their true colors, and I don't think I like it."

He went over to Coach Sammy. "I guess you're going to need a new point guard on your team," Dominic said.

"Looks like it," Coach Sammy replied.

"I'm not as fast as Lew, probably," Dominic said,

"but I have a pretty good shot from outside."

Coach Sammy looked at him with wide eyes.

"So what do you say?" Dominic said. "Can I join the Wasps?"

CHAPTER 8

THE BIG SWITCH

"Nothing in the rules against it," the ref said to Dominic. "If the Waverunners want to remove you from their lineup, they can. Once you're off the team, you can join the Wasps—since the Wasps are a community team."

"So we can have any team members we want," Sammy said.

"As long as they're middle school students somewhere, yes," the ref said.

Dominic walked over to the Waverunners' coach

and stood face-to-face with him. Coach Jenssen put his hands on the boy's shoulders. "If you do this," he said, "you won't be welcome back with the Waverunners again."

"That's fine with me," Dominic said. "I don't want to be on a team with guys who would be so nasty to the Wasps."

The coach held his gaze for a moment. He nodded. "All right," he said, turning to the scorekeepers' table. "Dominic is off the team."

With that, Coach Jenssen turned his back on Dominic and joined the other Waverunners at the visitors' bench.

Lew stepped up to Dominic. "That was pretty cool," he said. He put out his fist. "Glad to have you on the team."

Dominic bumped his fist. "Thanks," he said. "I should have joined right away. I knew a lot of the Waverunners were snobs. But my brother was a Waverunner at White Rock. So was my dad."

"Yeah, well," Lew said, "the Wasps didn't exist back then."

Dominic laughed. "Go get changed before the ref kicks you out of the building," he said. "Oh, and can I borrow your jersey?"

* * *

Dominic played for the whole fourth quarter. He wore Lew's jersey with a piece of tape over the name *Garrison*, with *Davis* written in black marker.

Lew sat in the front of the stands and watched. It felt weird to watch his best friends play basketball without him. He'd never really seen the Wasps move around the court from this angle before.

Nico passed the ball in to Dominic, who took the ball to the top of the key and passed it to Anang.

Anang got it to Nico for an easy two points from the post.

The Waverunners pushed hard. Lew could tell

the other boys from White Rock were eager to prove
to Dominic that he'd made a mistake in quitting the
team.

Their center controlled the ball at the top of the
key. He fired off a chest pass to their shooting guard
on the right wing. That player sank a three-pointer,
bringing the game within one basket.

Dominic led his new teammates in a drive with
less than a minute on the clock. He got the ball to their
small forward, who cut across the key and tried for a
hook shot.

He missed. Silas's replacement grabbed the
rebound and fired it off to Dominic's replacement. He
went straight for the hoop and tied the game.

Anang threw the ball in to Dominic at the top
of the key. Dominic faked a pass to Nico and drove
for the basket.

He went up for the layup through a crowded post.
The defense was all over him. The ball kissed the
backboard and dropped in for two.

The ref blew her whistle. "Foul," she said. "One shot."

"This will win the game for us," Lew said to himself. He wished so badly he was still in the game. It should be him taking this shot.

But Dominic was a great player, and free throws were his specialty.

"You got this," Nico said, clapping. He was the tallest kid lined up along the key. If Dominic missed, Nico's rebound could be the game-winner.

Lew was on the edge of his seat. He wished he could jump up and take Dominic's spot on the free throw line. Why did he have to lose his temper so easily?

He watched Dominic spin the ball, dribble it, and line up the shot. Dominic raised the ball and let it fly.

Swish!

The Wasps took the lead by one point. With only a few seconds left, the Waverunners threw the ball in and broke fast down the court. But there was no getting through.

The Waverunners' center heaved a shot from midcourt. It hit the backboard and bounced off, right into Nico's hands.

The buzzer rang.

The Wasps had won the game! But everyone assumed the Waverunners would take their spot in the finals.

CHAPTER 9

GOOD NEWS

After the game, the Wasps met up at Judy's Pizza, not far from the Westside Community Center.

"How'd our local boys do today?" said Judy as she delivered three large pizzas to their table.

"We won," Lew said, putting his chin on his fist. The rest of the boys at the table looked just as down as he did.

"Oh, I see," Judy said. "That would explain why you all look so happy."

Lew glared at her.

"Kidding, kidding," Judy said.

"We won the semifinals, but we won't be able to play in the finals," Nico explained.

"It's kind of a long story," Anang said.

"We're broke," Lew said.

"Okay, maybe not that long," Anang said with a shrug.

"We'd be happy to sponsor your team, if it'll help," said Judy.

"I'm afraid it's not that simple," Coach Sammy said. "With no community center, we won't even have a home court. That will disqualify us from the league."

Judy nodded. "Oh, I heard about the center closing," she said. "That's really a shame." She headed back to the kitchen.

Just then, Dominic came into the pizzeria, along with his parents.

"Sorry I'm late," Dominic said. "That is, if it's okay if I join you guys."

"Of course," Lew said. He scooted his chair over as Dominic pulled up a chair from a nearby table. "You're a Wasp now. Or you will be for a little while, since the Wasps are just about dead."

Dominic's mom stepped up to the table.

"Hi, Mrs. Davis," the boys said.

Coach Sammy stood up and shook her hand.

"There's a reason Dominic was late to your after-party," Mrs. Davis said to the team. "He and I sat in the car in the parking lot talking about the Wasps, the Waverunners, and the Westside Community Center."

"What about them?" Lew said.

"Well, you know that scoreboard I told you guys about the other day?" Dominic said. "The fancy one with four screens and all that?"

The Wasps nodded.

"My mom is paying for it," Dominic said.

"Not exactly," his mom said. "Besides being CEO at Davis Logistics, I also chair the board at the Davis Foundation."

"That's a big charity," Dominic said.

"We're a nonprofit investment group," she explained. "We invest in nonprofit enterprises around the city, and we donate to local organizations, schools, and the like."

"Such as White Rock Academy?" Coach Sammy said.

"Well, yes," she said, a little embarrassed. "Or we were planning to until tonight."

"Mom and I were so disappointed in the Waverunners' behavior tonight," Dominic said. "So I convinced Mom to use the funding for the new scoreboard for the community center instead."

Lew's mouth dropped open. "For real?" he said.

The others were shocked.

Coach Sammy stood up and stammered, "I don't know what to say. . . ."

"You don't have to say anything," Mrs. Davis said. "I've spoken with the foundation's attorney and accountants. They're on the phone with the community center board right now. With any luck," she finished, "this will be taken care of by morning."

"And that means the Wasps will be in the finals," Dominic said. He took a slice from the pepperoni pizza and enjoyed a big bite.

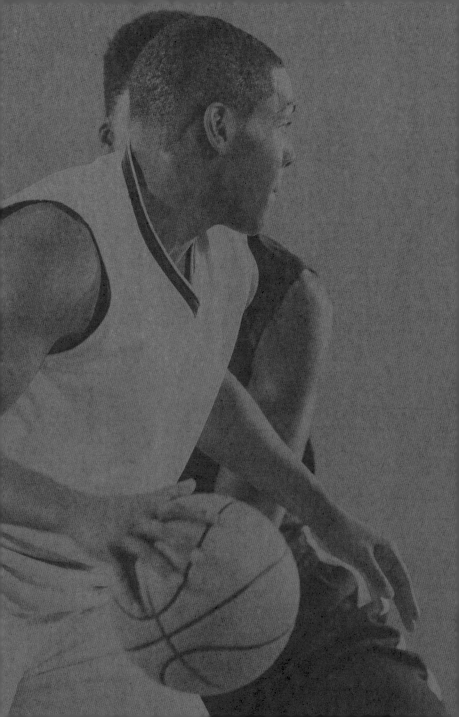

CHAPTER 10

ROCK CREEK RIVALRY

The money from the Davis Foundation, plus the few hundred dollars that Lew, Nico, and Anang managed to earn selling treats, was enough. The center would be able to pay all its back fees to the league and stay open.

The final game was Saturday night at Rock Creek Middle School against the Rockets.

"I can't wait to beat these guys," Lew said in the locker room huddle before the game.

Dominic bounced on his toes, raring to go. Today

he wore his own Wasps jersey, officially a member of the team.

"Since Dominic has such a strong outside shot," Coach Sammy said, "watch for Lew to call for plays that keep the ball around the three-point line.

"Nico," he went on, "you'll stay posted up, of course. The Rockets are tough at the boards, so I'm going to want to see Anang and Bonsa crowding out the paint as well on offense.

"Lew," Coach Sammy continued, "take advantage of that ball handling. They're a tough team but we're smarter and smoother."

Coach Sammy put his hand into the huddle. The boys did too.

"Goooo . . . ," they said together, "Wasps!"

* * *

"Introducing Westside Community Center," the announcer said over the speaker, "which we're all happy to learn has been saved by the Davis Foundation. That means this great team of boys can join us at the finals today. Please welcome the Wasps!"

The team jogged out from the locker hallway, and the five starters—Lew, Dominic, Anang, Bonsa, and Nico—took the court for a quick warmup.

"And your home team," the announcer went on, "the Rock Creek Rockets!"

The crowd went crazy. The Wasps had family and friends there, of course, but the Rockets had what looked like their whole middle school in the stands.

Lew tried to keep his mind on the drills he and his teammates were running, but the announcer went on to name every member of the Rock Creek Middle School team.

It was hard to focus. He kept watching the Rockets as they jogged in and high-fived each other.

"Let's keep our mind in the game," Coach Sammy said, clapping loudly right next to Lew.

"Sorry, Coach," Lew said.

"Keeping that temper in check today?" Sammy asked, more quietly.

Lew nodded. "Definitely," he said. "I'm not planning on spending the final game on the bench."

Sammy patted his shoulder as the lead referee blew her whistle. "Let's play some basketball," she called out.

The boys got into position for the tip-off. Nico faced the tallest Rocket, an eighth grader named Jasper.

The ref tossed the ball up. Nico seemed to launch halfway to orbit. He got a full hand on the ball and knocked it to Dominic on his right.

Dominic brought it up the court and found Lew at the top of the three-point line.

Nico posted up. Anang and Bonsa got into position on the wings, making cuts into the paint.

Nico was double guarded. Anang and Bonsa cut across, switching positions. Dominic rolled around behind Lew.

Lew faked a pass to Dominic and drove down the right side of the key. He went for the shot, but halfway up found Anang at the foul line with a fast pass.

Anang shot and scored the first two points of the game.

"Keep it up, boys," Coach Sammy called, clapping.

The Rockets threw in the ball and set up a slow 2-3 offense. Nico fought at the post for position. Jasper elbowed and shoved, but Nico kept his size-twelve sneakers planted.

Dominic and Lew played tight at the top of the arc. Under pressure, the Rockets' guards were forced to stall.

Anang and Bonsa stayed close to the wing men.

Finally the Rockets' point guard faked a pass to Jasper and dodged past Lew. He slipped down the lane and went up for a shot.

Nico blocked it, and Dominic grabbed the ball out of the air.

Lew sprinted up the court. Dominic found him

with a baseball pass, and Lew laid it up for an easy two points.

"There it is!" Coach Sammy yelled. "Nice D. Nice coordination. Keep it up, Wasps!"

The Rockets' fans stayed quiet.

"At least they're not booing," Lew said as he high-fived Dominic and they headed back on D.

The Rockets threw in the ball to restart play. This time they moved fast. Their guards hurried down the court and found Jasper halfway up the lane. He pushed on, right through Nico, and put up two points.

The crowd went crazy. Jasper and the Rockets' point guard bumped chests.

It was awkward, since Jasper was so much taller. Lew laughed.

"Something funny, Wasp?" Jasper taunted.

Lew opened his mouth to reply, but stopped himself. He glanced at Coach Sammy, who shook his head.

Lew just smiled and took the throw-in from Anang. He raised his closed fist to call the play.

Dominic, Anang, and Bonsa fell together on the right side of the key, while Nico took post on the left.

Lew drove up the middle while Nico screened for him. But instead of going to the basket, he passed it to Dominic. That put every Wasp between Dominic and the Rockets, giving him an open three-point shot.

The ball fell in with a swish for three, bringing the score to 7–2.

"Great shot, Dominic!" Coach Sammy called.

"Yeah, great shot," said the Rockets' point guard, a seventh grader named Tommy. "Traitor."

"What?" Dominic said. He stepped toward Tommy. He looked ready to fight.

SECOND-HALF SLUMP

"Whoa, whoa," Lew said, grabbing Dominic's arm. "Let it go, man. He's just trying to get you angry."

"Well, it's working," Dominic said.

Lew glanced at Coach Sammy, who nodded at him and flashed a thumbs-up.

The Rockets drove hard to the lane. Tommy found their right wing man with a chest pass. He stepped to the hoop and faked a layup. Nico jumped up to block, and the wing man was able to pass to Jasper.

Jasper laid it up for an easy two points.

"You got played," Jasper said to Nico with a sneer.

Nico ignored him and threw in to Bonsa, who passed it along to Lew. Lew set up at the top of the arc. He found Dominic at once.

Dominic moved along the right side of the key and passed it back to Lew. He set up a screen for him, so Lew could roll around to the right and get the ball to Anang.

Anang went in for the layup. Jasper blocked it cleanly. Bonsa grabbed the rebound and put it up again. Jasper intercepted the shot in midflight and launched a pass to Tommy, already halfway back up the court.

Tommy went to the basket unchallenged. The game was within one point.

The Rockets played hard and strong the rest of the first half. When the teams hit the locker rooms for halftime, the score was tied.

The Wasps took the court for the second half.

They shot and passed around during the last few minutes of the halftime break.

Tommy stood on the center circle and taunted the Wasps. "You're gonna lose today," he said.

"Shouldn't you be drilling with your team?" Anang said.

Tommy shrugged.

Dominic stepped up to him.

Lew stood next to him, ready to make sure a fight did *not* go down.

"Well, look at this," Tommy said. "The charity case and the white knight."

"Talk as much smack as you want," Lew said. "You won't get me into a brawl today." He hoped this was true.

"Yeah, not any of us," Nico said, stepping next to his friend. "We're going to win clean and take home that trophy."

"Home to where?" Jasper said, leaning over Tommy. "To the community center?"

"Some home that is," Tommy said. The Rock Creek boys high-fived.

Lew pulled Nico and Dominic away. "Come on, let's just finish drills," he said through gritted teeth.

The ref started the second half with the tip-off. This time Jasper—his face red with competition—won it easily. He knocked it toward Tommy, who caught the ball with both hands and dribbled down the court.

He set up a 1-3-1 offense and got around Lew. Lew stumbled as he gave chase. Tommy found a wing man as he cut through the key.

The Rockets' player went in for the layup. Nico blocked it, but Jasper picked up the rebound and put it home.

The Rockets had the lead for the first time. The crowd went wild. Lew's heart sank. The second half wasn't off to a great start.

Lew watched the scoreboard and the clock. There was plenty of time left—plenty of time for him and

Dominic to cool off and for the Wasps to play their best and their smartest.

Lew coolly dribbled up the court. He set up at the top left of the arc and quickly found Dominic to his right.

Dominic dribbled and shuffled his feet, his back to Tommy. He struggled to roll around him and got blocked at every turn. Lew could see the frustration on his new teammate's face.

Lew ran behind Dominic. "Give it here," Lew said.

Dominic fired a pass to him, then quickly set a pick on Lew's defender. Lew used the screen to lose his defender. He drove toward the basket and found Nico's big hands up and clear.

He lobbed the ball right into Nico's hands, but Jasper grunted and blocked his shot. Then he knocked the rebound loose, off Anang's knee, and out of bounds.

Nico shouted, "Come on!" His face was red with anger.

Tommy threw in to a small forward, who passed the ball to Jasper under the boards. Jasper went up, cleared Nico's block, and dropped in the two points.

"Guys, stay cool out here," Lew said as he took the throw-in from Bonsa.

He dribbled up the court and passed the ball to Dominic at the top of the key. Dominic rolled to the right, but he mis-dribbled. The ball bounced off his foot. "Arrgh!" Dominic shouted, furious with himself.

Tommy grabbed it and drove fast down the court.

Lew chased him, but Tommy got the layup for another two points. The score was 48–36.

The Rockets' lead was growing.

Bonsa threw in to Lew, and Lew immediately called time-out.

The ref blew her whistle, and Lew jogged to the bench.

"Coach," Lew said, "we're losing it out here."

"I've noticed," Coach Sammy replied.

The rest of the team jogged into a huddle with Lew and the coach. "Why'd you call time-out?" Dominic asked.

"Because we're beating ourselves out there," Lew said.

"Pretty sure they're beating us," Nico said. "That was Jasper who blocked my shot."

"And that was Tommy who stole it from me on the last drive," Dominic said.

"But you shouldn't have taken that shot," Lew said to Nico. "Jasper was in your face."

He turned to Dominic. "And you dribbled off your own foot," Lew said.

Dominic's face went red. He started to protest.

"You did," Anang said. "I saw that."

Dominic gritted his teeth, but he didn't argue.

"We need to stay cool out there," Lew said. "They're bigger and stronger than we are. If we play their game, we'll lose."

"So what game should we play?" Dominic asked Lew.

"*Our* game," Lew said. "Smart, cool, and quick. If we don't let them get to us and make us angry, we can focus on our play."

"Let's play some basketball, guys," the lead ref said. She blew her whistle.

* * *

Lew took control of the ball at the top of the key. Dominic took position outside the three-point line. Nico posted up, and Anang and Bonsa set up alongside the key.

Bonsa screened for Anang as Anang cut across the paint.

Lew passed to Anang, but Jasper was in his face right away.

Anang faked a jump shot and passed to Dominic, who got the ball back to Lew.

"Nice job, boys," the coach called from the sideline. "Keep your cool. Play it smart."

Anang cut back across the paint, and Lew faked the pass back to him. Jasper went with Anang to defend, but Lew drove along the left side of the key and went to the hoop. The basket was open for the easy two.

"Nice and easy, Lew!" Coach Sammy called, clapping.

"That's the last time that'll work, charity case," Jasper said as he hurried downcourt to post up on offense.

Lew ignored him and pressed hard on Tommy's point position.

Tommy raised two fingers. Lew heard the squeak of sneakers on the court behind him. He kept his eyes on Tommy's middle as the Rockets' point guard faked pass after pass. He faked a drive to the right, but it didn't fool Lew.

When he cut to the left, Lew kept on him like

butter on toast. Tommy got held up outside the lane and faded back across the three-point line.

Tommy tried to find an open man posted up, but Lew's teammates were playing close and smart. Tommy tried to find Jasper with a chest pass, but he panicked.

Lew was ready. He snatched the pass from midair, took two steps past Tommy, and found Dominic on the fast break to the hoop.

Lew launched the pass. Dominic took the pass into a dribble and went for the hoop. He laid it in for another two points.

"Call that foul, ref!" Tommy shouted.

"I didn't touch you!" Lew complained.

But Nico put a hand on his back. "Chill, chill," Nico said.

The ref shook her head. *No foul.*

"He's just trying to make you angry. Don't let it get to you," Nico said.

Lew nodded. "Thanks," he said.

"Come on, ref!" Tommy said.

"Now it's their turn to lose their cool," Dominic said quietly to Lew and Nico as the Rockets threw the ball in.

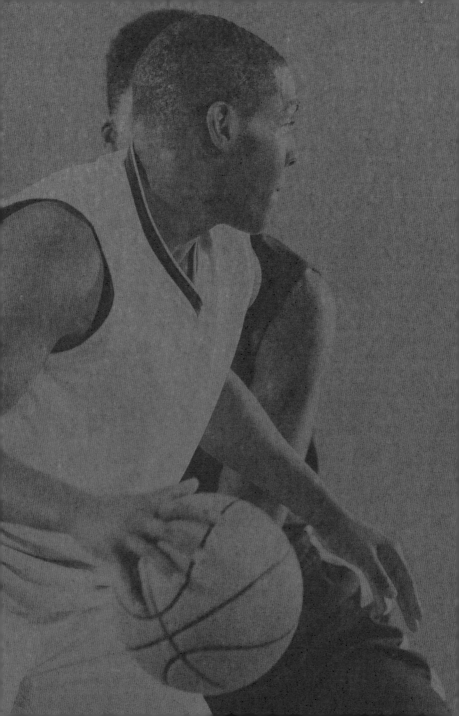

CHAPTER 12

THE LOVE OF THE GAME

The Rockets never got back their cool. They pushed hard and made mistakes.

The Wasps' spirit lifted, and with a minute left, with both teams out of time-outs, the Rockets led 60–58.

The Wasps took a last drive up the court. Lew set up, found Dominic with a bounce pass, and rolled to the left. With Nico posted up for a rebound, and Anang and Bonsa working to lose their defenders in the paint, Dominic faded to the top of the arc.

Lew came around behind him, took the handoff, and screened for Dominic.

Dominic was open where the three-point arc met the baseline.

Lew fired a chest pass to him. Dominic faked the shot with ten seconds left on the clock. Jasper jumped to block it, and Dominic took the shot when Jasper was on the way back down.

The ball struck the rim and bounced out.

Nico grabbed the rebound and passed it back to Lew at the top of the key.

Lew drove hard to the basket. Jasper and Tommy both went in for the block. Lew felt two arms bump his own as he rolled up an underhand layup.

It dropped in easily. Two points.

The ref blew her whistle. "And one," she said. There were just four seconds left on the clock.

Lew would get one foul shot. If he made it, the Wasps' victory was all but sealed.

Jasper and another Rockets player took the

positions at post. If Lew missed, they could grab the rebound and might get another shot to take the lead back.

If Lew made the basket, it would give the Wasps a one-point lead.

"Don't blow it, charity boy," Tommy said. He stood in the spot just to Lew's right, ready to block him from getting a rebound if he missed.

Lew smiled. Tommy had been trying the whole second half to make him angry, and it hadn't worked.

"It's over," Lew said. He raised the ball and let it soar. It fell in with a swish.

The Wasps fell back on D as Jasper threw in to Tommy. Tommy launched a wild shot from half court. It wasn't even close.

The buzzer went off, the ref blew her whistle, and the Wasps fell into a celebration huddle at center court.

* * *

At Judy's Pizza after the game, the Wasps pushed five tables together. Coach Sammy, all the players, and everyone's friends and families crowded together for celebration pizza and soda.

The trophies stood in a group in the center of the table, shiny and golden, a figure in mid-hook shot with the ball held high.

"I'm proud of you boys," Coach Sammy said. "You took control of that game tonight."

"Thanks, Coach," Lew said.

"You really led us today, Lew," Nico said.

Dominic nodded. "You helped me keep my cool, for sure," he said.

"And you both had my back when I needed it," Lew said to Nico and Dominic.

Dominic's mother stood up and raised her glass of soda. Everyone went quiet.

"A toast to the Wasps," she said, "a group of boys who proved today that our foundation made the right choice of what team to sponsor."

Everyone raised their cups.

"And they showed that we don't play to win,"
she went on. "We play for our team and community."

"And we play for the love of the game," Anang
said.

"We play our best," said Dominic.

"Especially when we've got a home court!"
said Lew.

Everyone cheered.

ABOUT the AUTHOR

Steve Brezenoff is the author of more than fifty middle-grade chapter books, including the Field Trip Mysteries series, the Ravens Pass series of thrillers, and the Return to the Titanic series. He's also written three young-adult novels, *Guy in Real Life*; *Brooklyn, Burning*; and *The Absolute Value of –1*. In his spare time, he enjoys video games, cycling, and cooking. Steve lives in Minneapolis with his wife, Beth, and their son and daughter.

GLOSSARY

brawl (BRAWL)—a rough or noisy fight

cease (SEES)—to stop or come to an end

eject (i-JEKT)—to force someone to leave

embarrassment (em-BAR-uhs-muhnt)—the feeling of being ashamed

foundation (foun-DAY-shuhn)—an organization that gives money to good causes

huddle (HUHD-uhl)—a gathering of players on a team before a play

hydrate (HYE-drayt)—to achieve a healthy balance of fluids in the body

loudmouth (LOUD-mouth)—a person who talks too much and has unpleasant things to say

precinct (PREE-singkt)—a police station in a particular area of a city or town

rickety (RIK-i-tee)—poorly made and likely to break

sponsor (SPON-sur)—a person or organization that finances a program or activity carried out by another

vertical (VUR-tuh-kuhl)—straight up and down

DISCUSSION QUESTIONS

1. Explain how Lew acts when he finds out that the team might not continue to exist. Discuss why you think he reacts the way he does.

2. Which of Lew's qualities do you think are good characteristics? How does Lew demonstrate these qualities? Give examples from the text.

3. Describe the setting of the story. How did the author help you understand the setting?

WRITING PROMPTS

1. Pretend you are a local newspaper reporter. Write an article covering the finals game between the Wasps and the Rockets.

2. In Chapter 6, Lew has to face his friend Dominic head-to-head in a playoff game. Have you ever competed against a friend? Write a paragraph or two about what it was like.

3. Pick a scene in which you disagreed with how a character handled a situation. An example could be when Lew loses his temper with an opposing team. Rewrite the scene the way you think it should have happened.

MORE ABOUT POINT GUARDS

Point guards are one of five positions on a basketball team. The other positions are shooting guards, small forwards, power forwards, and centers.

Point guards are considered leaders on the court. They must have good ball-handling skills, such as dribbling and passing. They often decide which plays the team is going to run, so they must be good decision-makers.

Because they often call the plays, the point guard should understand the coach's strategy and set the team up to accomplish it on the court.

Who was the greatest point guard of all time? Many people believe it was Magic Johnson, who played for the Los Angeles Lakers for thirteen seasons. He led his team to five National Basketball Association (NBA) championships during his time on the Lakers. Johnson retired from the NBA in 1991.

Another famous point guard is Stephen Curry, who plays for the Golden State Warriors. He is a three-time NBA champion and two-time NBA Most Valuable Player.

Point guards are often the shortest people on the court. The average height of NBA point guards is around 6 feet, 3 inches. The average height of NBA players in general is around 6 feet, 7 inches.

FOR MORE
ACTION ON THE COURT,
PICK UP . . .

JAKE MADDOX JV

BAD-LUCK
BASKETBALL

JAKE MADDOX JV

FREE THROW
FAIL